A QUESTION OF YAMS

A missionary story based on true events
by Gloria Repp

journey**forth**®

Greenville, South Carolina

Library of Congress Cataloging-in-Publication Data:
Repp, Gloria, 1941–
    A question of yams / Gloria Repp ; illustrated by Roger Bruckner.
    Summary: After his father plants the family yam garden without praying to the ancestor spirits, Kuri, a young boy of Papua New Guinea, wonders if he should follow the advice of the Christian missionaries and trust in their God.
    ISBN 0-89084-614-6
    [1. Papua New Guinea—Fiction. 2. Missionaries—Fiction. 3. Christian life—Fiction.] I. Bruckner, Roger, 1949– ill. II. Title.
    PZ7.R296QU   1992   91-45761
    [E]—dc20   CIP
                                                         AC

A Question of Yams

Edited by Karen Daniels

© 1992 by BJU Press
Greenville, South Carolina 29614
JourneyForth Books is a division of BJU Press

ISBN 978-0-89084-614-8

20   19   18   17

For Sjaan and John Waller,
who have given their lives
to the work of Bible translation.

Acknowledgments

My sincere thanks to the following for their help
in ensuring the accuracy of this story:

Kim Beaty
Roger Garland
Terry Whalin

and Mrs. Jaki Parlier, who generously shared
her experiences as a missionary-translator
in Papua New Guinea and
checked the final manuscript.

G. R.

Contents

Books by Gloria Repp

The Secret of the Golden Cowrie

The Stolen Years

Night Flight

A Question of Yams

Publisher's Note

Kuri's story is based on the experiences of Amok, a Christian man of Papua New Guinea who dared to defy the traditions of the yam cult. Amok's people believed that their gardens, on which their lives depended, would not produce unless they prayed to ancestor spirits and practiced certain magical rites.

In Kuri's village, his father had come to know the true God when he helped the missionaries learn his language and begin translating the words of "God's Carving," the Bible.

From his father's steadfast reliance on God, Kuri *(KOO-ree)* learns the meaning of faith. At the same time, opposition from the village leaders and the ridicule endured by his family teach him to find his peace in God alone. Kuri's spiritual growth as he reads the Bible in his own tongue reminds us of the need for every tribe and nation to hear the life-giving Word.

Despite their uneasy circumstances, God blesses Kuri's family in many ways. Even so, one question still remains in Kuri's mind, a question about the yam soup that had always been his favorite. In His answer, God demonstrates His understanding of small matters and His concern for the heart of a young boy.

> *"Behold, God is mighty, and despiseth not any:*
> *he is mighty in strength and wisdom."*
> Job 36:5

1
Waiting

Kuri ran down the path,
his bare feet quick and light.
He crossed a wide stream
by leaping from stone to stone.

Then he followed the path
halfway up a hill, turned,
and ducked into the bushes.

Just a few steps into the jungle
stood his favorite rock.

He scrambled up onto
its rough grey top.
Thick bushes grew on all sides,
and branches hung low over it.
He was hidden here,
as hidden as a possum
in the treetops.

From the rock,
he could see the path
and past it to his family's garden.
The mounds of brown earth
in the garden
were ready for planting.

Father would be here soon.
All he had to do was wait.

A breeze stirred the nearby leaves.
Parrots called to each other
from the trees that arched above him.
But Kuri kept his eyes on the path.

Was Father really
going to plant the garden
without praying to the spirits?
He had never done such a thing before.

Maybe it was
because of the missionaries.

Father had been
helping the missionaries
with their work.
Maybe he had listened too much
to their talk.

Kuri craned his neck
to look down the path.
He ducked back.
Father was coming with the yams.

He peered through the leaves again.
Father had reached the garden,
but three men followed
close behind him.
The Head Men!
What were they so angry about?

They stood in the garden,
muttering to each other.

Then the one named Sakoso spoke up.
He had grey hair and a loud voice.
"You must pray to the spirits
before you plant the yams.
If you don't, you will be sorry."

Father put the yams
down on the ground and
began to dig with his stick.

Sakoso glared at him.
"Something bad will happen
to your garden. Wait and see."

Kuri shivered in his hiding place.

But Father did not seem afraid.
"I will not beg the spirits for help,"
he said. "I will trust the mighty God.
And I will plant our yams
in the name of Jesus Christ."

He bowed his head,
and Kuri knew that his father
was praying to God.

The Head Men stared at Father.
They turned and went back up the path.

Kuri stayed on the rock
to think for a while.
Last year Father had often
prayed to the spirits.
But one day two missionary ladies
came to live near their village.

"We want to learn your language,"
the missionaries said to Father.

So Father began
helping them with words.
"What is this?" the ladies would ask.
"What is that?"

And Father would tell them
the right word to say.

The missionaries read to Father
from God's Carving.
They said it was full of God's talk.

Father began to tell Kuri
about the words in God's Carving.
"Behold, God is mighty,"
Father said over and over.
It was the part of God's Carving
that he liked best.

After a while, Father stopped
praying to the spirits.
Kuri didn't know if that
was good or not.

The Head Men wanted everyone
to pray to the spirits.
The spirits were powerful, and
the Head Men knew how to please them.
But Father said he would trust
in God, not the spirits.

Kuri shook his head.
How strong was Father's God?

2
The Head Men

That night, the Christians
met at Kuri's house.
There weren't very many of them.
The missionary ladies,
Anne and Joyce, came too.

Joyce was a tall lady
with yellow hair and a sunburned face.
She read some words from God's Carving;
then Kuri's father spoke to the men.

"Pray with us," he said.
"I have planted my yams
in the Christian way.
So have two others."

"Aren't you afraid?"

asked one of the men in a low voice.

"No," said Kuri's father.

"The spirits cannot make the crops grow.

We cannot make the crops grow.

Only God can do that.

God's Carving says,

Behold, God is mighty.

He is mighty in strength and wisdom."

The Christians prayed
for a long time that night.
When Kuri grew tired,
he curled up on his mat
and gazed at the smoky fire.

I wish we had planted the yams
the way we used to, he thought.
How can Father be so sure
about his God?
What is going to happen to us?

Every day after that,
Kuri went down to the garden
to see how the yams were doing.

One morning he found sprouts,
tender and green, poking up
from the earth. He shouted
the news to his family.

"The yams have come up!
Every one of them is sprouting!"

"Thank God," Father said
with a smile. "Behold, He is mighty!"

But that night the Head Men
paid Kuri's family a visit.
"Hear my words," said Sakoso.

"You should plant the yams
the way our fathers did."

His voice grew louder.
"The spirits will be angry and punish you.

Maybe they will punish all of us."
He stared right at Kuri's father.
"Even if your yams have sprouted,
they will die.
Then you will go hungry."

The Head Men left,
and Kuri looked to see
if his father was worried.

Father's dark eyes
held only sadness.
"We must pray more
for those men," he said.
"If they knew the power of God,
they would believe.
But He will show them. He is mighty."

The next morning,
Kuri ran down to the garden.
He knelt by the little plants,
afraid that they would be
wilted and brown.
But they were still green,
and they looked taller than ever.

Day after day, the sun warmed
the little plants.
Day after day, the rain watered them,
as it always did.

Soon, bright green vines
began to creep across the mounds.
Kuri's mother weeded the vines
and used her hoe to break up
the soil around them.

After a while,
Kuri began to think more about
hunting wild pigs than about yams.
One day he and Father
had just started out
when Sakoso stopped them.

"Your yams may still grow,
but they will not live long,"
Sakoso warned.
His eyes looked like black slits
in his wrinkled brown face.
"The spirits will punish you
and your family—soon."

Kuri stood still
as the Head Man walked off.
Why was Sakoso so sure
that something bad would happen?
He decided to keep a closer watch
on their garden.

3
The Shadow

The next day, Kuri went fishing.
When he came back along the stream,
he heard voices.
Some men must be talking
on the other side of the water.
Who were they?

He ducked into the bushes
at the edge of the stream.
Slowly and quietly,
he slipped from bush to bush.
Someone said his father's name.

He crept closer and closer
until he could see two men
behind a pile of rocks.
He caught sight of gray hair.
Sakoso! What was he saying
about Father?

Kuri did not stir.
Sakoso was talking to a man
who was as thin as a shadow,
a man Kuri had never seen before.

Then Kuri heard just a few words:
". . . and he must be punished . . ."
After that, Sakoso began to whisper.
A minute later, the thin man nodded
and ran off.

Kuri crept back to the path
and headed toward the garden.

Once again he hid on the rock
behind the tall bushes,
and he waited.

He listened to the noisy birds.
He swatted at the flies
that buzzed around his head.
He waited and waited.

The sun began to set,
making long shadows
that slid across the garden.
Kuri yawned. Maybe he had been wrong
about the thin man.

He peered through the
leaves again, and another yawn
died in his throat.

One of those shadows in the garden
was a man. It was the thin man,
and he held a long, knobby stick
in his hands.

Kuri jumped down off the rock.

The thin man raised his stick;
he swung it down onto the yam vines.

Kuri snatched up stones
and threw them, hard.
He rushed from his hiding place.
"No! No! Stop it!" he shouted.

He looked up the path.

"Come everyone! Come and see
the wicked man in our garden."
He yelled as loudly as he could.

The thin man ran away
just as Father hurried down the path.

"That man tried to
beat down our yams," Kuri cried.
"I heard Sakoso telling him what to do.
The Head Men must have sent him
to ruin our garden."

To Kuri's surprise,
Father bowed his head.
He stood right there in the garden
and asked God to protect their yams.
Then he added, "Mighty God,
You have seen the men
who want to do this wicked thing.
Show them Your power."

Kuri had never heard Father
pray in such a loud voice.
He hoped the thin man was listening.

His father turned to him with a smile. "Thank God that you were here, my son."

4
A Small Red Mark

Kuri went to cut some firewood,
and he thought about what he had seen.

God had kept their garden safe,
even though the Head Men
wanted to ruin it.
But why had they tried to
destroy the yams?
Maybe they were not sure
that the spirits would punish Father.

As he reached down into the grass,
Kuri felt a stab of pain.

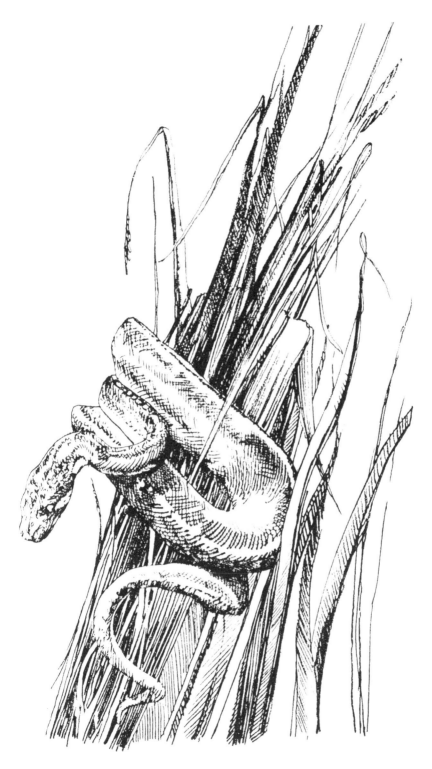

27

He jerked his hand back.
There on his thumb
was a small red mark
—the bite of a snake.

He stared at the red mark,
feeling suddenly ill.
Now he would die.

He left his axe
and stumbled toward his house.

Near the house, he met Father.
Kuri held out his hand.
"A snake—it bit me!"

Father bent over Kuri's hand.
Already it was starting to swell.
"Sit down," he said. "Don't move.
I'll go get one of the missionaries."

Kuri leaned against the house
and gazed at his hand.
A small boy wandered past,
then stopped to look at it too.
His eyes widened.
He threw a glance at Kuri's face
and ran off to tell the village.

Soon Father was back with Joyce.

Kuri was not afraid
of the tall missionary,
even though she had white skin.
Sometimes, after Father finished
helping Joyce with words,
she would tell them both a story
from God's Carving.

She took Kuri's hand
in her own.

"What kind of snake bit you?
Do you know?"

He shook his head,
wishing he had seen it.

But she did not seem upset.
"Kuri, you just lie down on your mat
and keep still.
I called the doctor on the radio.
He'll be here as soon as he can,
and he'll bring some medicine
that's good for snake bites."

She glanced at the dark clouds
that hung low in the sky.
"Let's pray that the clouds open up
so the helicopter can get here."

Kuri watched her yellow hair
through half-closed eyes.

She nodded at his father.

"I'll get some men to pray," Father said.

Kuri's mother sat down
next to him, weeping softly.
The Christians came into the house
and stood around his mat.
They began to pray.

Other people crowded in,
and Kuri heard them whispering.
"That boy—
his father planted their garden
in the Christian way.
Look what happened to him.
Surely he is being punished."

Kuri's eyes flew open in alarm.

"Don't worry about them,"
Father said.
"You trust God, Kuri.
We have talked to Him about this,
and He will take care of you."

Kuri tried to lift his hand,
but it felt too heavy.
He tried to move his feet,
but they were numb.

"Bring nettles," he said.
"I cannot feel my feet.
They are dying."

His mother jumped up
to get some stinging nettles.
But even when she rubbed
the green plants across his feet,
Kuri could feel nothing.

He wanted to ask
if he were going to die,
but he was too tired to say the words.
He gazed at Father's face.
It was calm, just as it had been
when he faced the Head Men.

Kuri thought about Sakoso's threats
and the Head Men's wicked plans.

"Father is wise to trust
in the mighty God," he told himself.
And he closed his eyes.

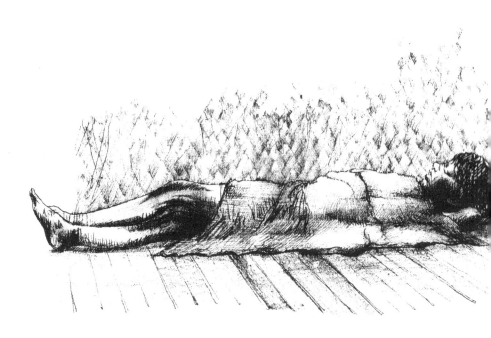

5
Too Dry

Kuri awoke with a jerk,
wondering at the noise outside.
It was as loud as thunder.
Father stood in the doorway,
looking off toward the mountains.

But it wasn't thunder—
it was the sound of the noisy bird
that Joyce called a helicopter.
The doctor must be coming.

Before long, a white man
was bending over him.
Kuri felt a prick in his arm,
like the prick of a thorn.

The doctor stood up.
"That might do it," he said
to Kuri's father.
"The Lord sure answered prayer.
He got us through those clouds."

Father smiled,
then he glanced back at Kuri.
"We have prayed, and
God will do as He wishes.
Thank you for coming to help."

He went outside with the doctor.
"I have some coconuts here for you.
And I want to give some to the pilot
of the helicopter."

The next time
Kuri opened his eyes,
he felt better.
Soon he could leave his mat
and sit in front of his house.

He blinked in the sunlight.
He could feel its warm rays seeping
into his bones, making him strong.

One morning
as Kuri sat in the sun,
he saw that the ground
was dry and cracked.
Isn't this the rainy season? he thought.
The sun has been shining for many days.
Too many days.

What about the yams?
They would die without rain.

Kuri pulled himself to his feet.
Father hadn't said much
about the garden lately.
But the Christians
had been praying more than ever.

He plodded down to see the yams.
It seemed like a long way,
and his breath was coming fast
by the time he got there.

The plants were still green,
but the vines had not even
spread across the mounds.
Their curly ends seemed to droop,
and their leaves were much too small.

Kuri sighed.
The yams had to get some rain soon,
or they would die.

He dragged himself back up the path
and slid to the ground in front of his house.
He leaned back, closing his eyes
against the hot sun.

Some women walked by,
and he listened to their chatter.
Their gardens were dry too.
They were going to ask the Head Men
to make it rain.

Then he heard his father's
cheerful voice,
and it filled him with hope.
He swallowed the dusty feeling
in his throat.
Maybe God would send rain.
Maybe it wasn't too late for the yams.

That night, the Christians
came to pray again.
After they left, Kuri asked his father,
"What about the yams? What if they die?
Will you plant them the Christian way
next time?"

His father looked deep
into Kuri's eyes.
"God will do what He wants to
about the rain. Perhaps He will
give us a good crop of yams.

Perhaps not. He is the mighty One.
But even so, I will not go back
to the old ways."

He put a hand on Kuri's shoulder.
"You know that the Christians
prayed a lot when the snake bit you.
We have prayed a lot for our gardens,
and we have prayed for the Head Men."

Kuri nodded, remembering.

"We learned some good things
while we were talking to God,"
Father went on. "And we have grown
stronger in our hearts.
I would rather know God
than have ten houses
that are filled with yams."

Kuri felt something move
in his own heart, as if
a tiny green shoot were pushing up
through the crusted earth.
He looked at his father and thought,
A God who can make hearts strong
is mighty indeed.

"Father," he mumbled,
"I want to know God too."

His father's eyes gleamed.
"I have learned about God from the talk
in His Carving. Anne and Joyce
have helped me to understand it.
Tomorrow we will go and see them."

6
God's Carving

The next day, Father went
to help the missionaries,
and he took Kuri with him.

Joyce was bent over the table
where she did her work.
Father sat in a chair, and Kuri did too.
He stared at the floor and tried
to think of the right words to say.

After a while, Father said,
"My son wants to know God."

Kuri gave Joyce a quick glance.

He saw the smile in her eyes,
so he asked, "How can you tell
what God's talk is?"

"I see the words He gave us
in His Book."

He looked at the table.
"What words?"

She picked up something
that looked like a dry banana leaf.
It had rows of black marks on it.

"These are words," she said.
She pointed to the marks.
"I look at these words, and
I can hear what they say."

Kuri leaned across the table.
He stared hard at the black marks,
but they didn't say anything to him.

He turned to Joyce with a frown.

"I hear the words in my head
when I read them," she said quickly.

Kuri looked at his father.
"Can you read these words?"

"No." Father's voice was sad.
"When I see Joyce making God's Carving
in our talk, I want to read too.
But it will take me a long time;
I think my head is very hard."

After a minute he said,
"But you could learn right now."

Joyce smiled at them.
"You could both learn to read.
Kuri, I could begin teaching you today
if you really want to."

Later, when Kuri left Joyce's house,
he felt like singing.
She had talked to him some more
about Jesus Christ. Then they prayed.

After that, she had started to teach him
about the little black marks
on the dry banana leaf.

Kuri looked up at his father,
who walked quietly beside him.
"I think I like reading," he said.
"Now I know the marks for 'pig'
and 'father' and 'house'.
Maybe soon I will be able to read
God's Carving for myself."

His father shook his head,
but he had a smile on his face.
"There are many more words to learn.
Joyce has boxes and boxes of words.
But keep on, my son, and you will be glad."

They came to a fork in the path,
and Father turned toward the garden.
"Let's go this way," he said.
He stopped at the edge of the stream.
"Thank God that He has kept
this water from drying up.
If all the Christians work with us,
maybe our yams will still be good.
You can help too."

Soon Kuri was working harder
than he ever had in his whole life.

Every day he carried buckets
and buckets of water from the stream
all the way up the hill to the garden.

He dumped buckets and buckets of water
over the thirsty yam plants.

While he worked, he thought about
the words he was trying to learn.
Joyce had made the black marks
for his new words on
pieces of dry banana leaf
that she called "paper."
Then she had stuck the paper together
into a book.

Each book had words and pictures
that told a story.
Now Kuri could read
some of the books by himself.
One part of God's Carving
was a book named "Mark."
It was the book Kuri liked best.

The first time he read
from the book of Mark,
he ran all the way home.

"I read God's Carving today,"
he told his mother.
"I read it in our own words,
and I understood it with my heart,
not just my ears."

She smiled at him.
"Maybe you can read it to me too."

He smiled back. "Yes!
It tells about Jesus Christ,
the mighty Son of God.
Even the spirits obey Him."

His mother nodded.
"I would like to hear about that."

7
The Story of Job

For a long time,
the Christians helped each other
with their gardens.
The yam vines grew slowly,
but they didn't die.

It seemed odd to Kuri that
they had to water the plants,
because in other years
the rains had always come.

The people of the village
said it was odd too.

They shook their heads
when Father tried to tell them
about the buckets
the Christians were using.
They told him that they would wait
for the spirits to send rain.

And while they waited,
their gardens dried up.

Each day, Kuri looked to see
if there were any clouds in the sky.
At last he saw a long line
of heavy gray clouds
roll across the mountains.

Rain began to fall.
It fell harder and harder
until it looked like a
solid sheet of water.

The little stream became

a rushing brown river,

and every path was deep with mud.

But the rains came too late
for the village gardens.

The Head Men knew that
the Christians' gardens had not died.
When Sakoso spoke to Kuri's father,
his words were like stinging nettles.
He said that the spirits were still angry.

But now Kuri understood
how Father could be so calm.
He knew from God's Carving that
Jesus Christ had power
over the evil spirits.

The Head Men told the people
that the Christians' yams
might grow a little.
But even so,
they would surely taste bitter.

And Father told the Christians
again and again:
"God will take care of us.
Remember, His Carving says,
Behold, God is mighty."

When Kuri went to Joyce's house,
he asked her about Father's verse.
"Where is it in God's Carving?
I want to read it for myself."

Joyce took down
the thick black book that she
always kept by her table.
She opened it to a page near the middle.
Kuri bent over the page
and studied it.

He looked up at her.
"But I can't read this.
These aren't the words of my village."

Joyce nodded sadly.

"This is a part of God's Carving
that we haven't worked on yet."

"When will you get it done?"
asked Kuri.

"First we want to finish
the part about Jesus Christ
so the people can read about Him."

"Yes," Kuri agreed.
He tapped the page in front of him.
"And what is this part
of God's Carving called?"

"That's a story
about a man named Job."

Job? It sounded like
an odd name to Kuri,
but still he wanted to
read the story.

He started to ask,
"How long—?"

But he stopped when he saw
the look on Joyce's face.

For a minute he was silent.
"I'll help you!" he said at last.
"I'm learning to read
more and more. I'll learn faster.
I'll help you get the right words.
Someday I will read
the story of Job for myself."

Much later that day,
Kuri said good-bye to Joyce.
His head was tired from all
the words he had stuffed into it.
But Joyce had said he was doing well.
Perhaps I will know all the words soon,
he told himself.
Then I can start to help her.

He took a big breath of fresh air.
It felt good to be outside again.
Maybe he would go to the garden
and see how the yams were doing.

Now that the rains had come,
the plants were growing fast.
Each mound was covered with
curling vines and shiny green leaves.

Father had said it wouldn't be long
before the yams were ready to eat.

Kuri wished it were today.
He liked to eat roasted yams,
and he liked to eat boiled yams,
but he liked them best
in the good soup his mother made.

The Head Men were still saying
that the yams would be bitter.
He hoped not.
How would the soup taste then?

Slowly Kuri left the garden.
"Behold, God is mighty,"
he said to himself.
"I will not worry about the yams."

He began to think about
the new part of Mark
he had read that day.
Maybe he'd take it home
and read it to Mother too.

8
Bitter Yams?

At last the yams were ready
to dig up. All the Christians
came with their families.
The women and children brought
sticks to help with the digging.
Kuri stood with the men and watched.

The yams weren't very big,
but there were a lot of them.
Father stepped into the midst
of the dusty brown piles.

"Look at this!" he cried.
"We will have enough!

The mighty God has kept us
from going hungry.
He has answered our prayers."

Kuri's mother and the other women
loaded the yams into string bags
and carried them off.

Now for the soup, thought Kuri.

He saw his mother pick green onions
for the soup and chop them up.
She peeled the yams and cut them up too.

The water in her cooking pot
began to bubble,
so she stirred in the green onions
and the yams. She threw in
some salt and some ginger.
Then she cooked the soup
over the fire for a long time.

Will it taste like it did before?
Kuri asked himself. Will it be good?
But he didn't say the words out loud.

When they sat down to eat,
Father bowed his head over the soup.
He prayed a long prayer.

First he thanked God
for all He had done
to take care of the family
and the crop of yams.
Then he thanked God that
today Sakoso had asked him
some questions about God's Carving.

As Kuri listened,
he felt warm inside.
Maybe soon God would answer
Father's prayers for the Head Men.

When Father said "Amen,"
Kuri opened his eyes
and looked at his bowl.
Slowly he dipped his spoon
into the steaming soup.

It had orange chunks of yams in it,
and small green bits of onion,
and it was the best yam soup
he had ever tasted.

His father smiled at his mother,
and Kuri smiled with them.
God had given him words to read
and yam soup too.

"Thank God for such good soup,"
his father said. Kuri knew
what Father was going to say next,
and he joined in with all his heart.
"Behold, God is mighty!"

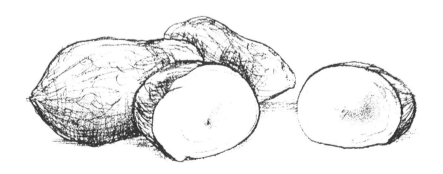